NO.1 BOY DETECTIVE

Under Cover

Barbara Mitchelhill

Illustrated by

Tony Ross

Andersen Press • London

To the children of St Dominic's Priory School, Stone,
who have a beautiful new library

This edition first published in 2017 by
Andersen Press Limited
20 Vauxhall Bridge Road
London SW1V 2SA
www.andersenpress.co.uk

First published by Andersen Press Limited in 2009

2 4 6 8 10 9 7 5 3

British Library Cataloguing in Publication Data available.

ISBN 978 1 78344 668 1

Printed and bound in Turkey by Omur Printing Co, Istanbul

Chapter 1

It was the Friday before half term.

'Guess what?' said Mum as if she was really pleased. 'We're going to spend the week at Green Park Holiday Village.'

'Do we have to?' I said. 'I want to stay at home and solve crimes. I was thinking of checking out the local bank for robbers.'

Mum didn't listen. 'The chef has been rushed into hospital, Damian, and they've asked me to do the cooking.'

'Hospital?' I said. 'What kind of excuse is that? My half term will be ruined.'

She couldn't see it. 'Treat it as a holiday,' she said. 'It'll be fun. There are lots of chalets built in a wood. And there's even a small swimming pool.'

It wasn't exactly Disney World but I suppose I could put up with it.

'OK, Mum. I'll go,' I said. 'I'll take my bike.'

But she shook her head. 'There won't be room in the van, Damian. I've got cakes and gateaux and quiches to bake tonight. It'll be packed full.'

She went on and on about how much work she had to do. And whenever I slipped the word 'bike' into the conversation, she just shouted, 'NO! NO! NO!'

The next morning, Mum was not in a good mood.

'WILL YOU PLEASE GET UP, DAMIAN!' she yelled from the kitchen.

'We've got to go in five minutes!'

Anyway, just to please her, I got dressed and went downstairs.

The van was in the drive with the back doors wide open. Mum had loaded it already and I noticed that there was still plenty of room for my bike. All I had to do was push the pies and cakes and quiches to one side.

I looked over my shoulder. Mum was busy locking up the house. There was time to sneak over to the shed and find my bike. Quick as I could, I wheeled it across to the van and lifted it into the back. With only a bit of shoving, it fitted snugly between the steak pies and the chocolate gateaux.

The deed was done. I slammed the doors shut knowing that Mum would never notice.

Chapter 2

By the time Mum came back, I was sitting in the passenger seat. As she climbed in, I smiled my Angel Smile. (I practise smiling in the mirror. It can be very useful with grown-ups.)

'Everything all right, Mum?' I asked in my kindly voice.

She didn't say anything. But she frowned as she turned on the engine. I think she was feeling sad. So, to make her feel better, I sang her a song called *Bad Boys on the Beat. Yeah! Yeah!*

'Thank you, Damian,' she snapped. 'Please be quiet. I've got a headache.'

'Just once more, Mum, and your headache will be gone. I promise.'

'NO, THANK YOU,' she said.

After that, I hummed ever so quietly under my breath and Mum gritted her teeth. I could see she was feeling better already.

It was bad luck that, halfway to the Holiday Village, we had to go up a hill. It was really, really steep and suddenly I heard a noise in the back of the van. A sort of sliding sound. Then a crashing like breaking china.

'What's that?' said Mum, slamming her foot on the brake. That was the worst thing she could have done 'cos everything slid the other way and crashed for the second time.

She jumped out, raced to the back of the van and flung open the doors. Well, she practically blew her top. Just

6

because my bike had fallen over and a few chocolate cakes were an intsy-wintsy bit squashed. I ask you! I even pointed out that they would taste just as good as they would in one piece. But she couldn't see it. She was in one of her big strops.

She didn't say another word all the way to Green Park. When we arrived, we drove through some iron gates, up a long drive and stopped outside a big wooden hut called the Cookin' Shack. This was the dining room where the holiday-makers ate and the kitchen where Mum was going to cook.

I have to say that Mum's mood didn't get any better that day. Even while I was helping to empty the van, she kept shouting, 'Be careful, Damian,' as I carried things through. 'Don't do that! Now look what you've done!' That kind of thing. I was doing my best.

According to Mr Grimethorpe, our teacher, child labour was abolished hundreds of years ago – but I don't think Mum knows this fact.

I was soon exhausted and I slipped outside for a break. I was sitting under a tree opening a bag of prawn cocktail crisps when I saw a boy riding a bike down the path. I couldn't believe my eyes.

It was none other than Calvin Baggington, known as Baggy-Pants. He was a new boy in our class and *not popular*! He was the boy who had everything – money, sweets, mobile phone and his own computer.

I couldn't stand him. He was always bragging. Saying how rich his dad was. Just my luck he'd come to the Holiday Village for half term.

Chapter 3

'Hi, Damian!' said Baggy-Pants as he raced nearer. He was wearing a brand new tracksuit – bright blue with white stripes – and a yellow and black helmet. Yuk!

'Hi,' I said unenthusiastically.

He jumped off his bike and pushed it across the grass towards me.

'Like my birthday present?' he said, pointing to the bike. It was red and silver with special gears and flashy bits and pieces that were quite unnecessary. He couldn't wait to tell me about them.

'My dad said I had to have the best. And I've got all the cycling gear, too. Shoes, gloves, waterproofs . . .'

Yak. Yak. Yak. It was really boring. I just kept eating the crisps.

Then Baggy-Pants spotted Mum's van with the words Home Cooking Unlimited on the side.

'So that's why you're here,' he said. 'Your mum's doing the catering, is she?'

I just grunted.

'Suppose you'll be doing the washing up, eh?'

I stayed cool. 'Me?' I said, raising my eyebrows. 'No.'

'Great,' he said. 'Then we can go riding together.'

I shook my head. 'I'll be working.'

'Working?' he said.

I opened my mouth and dropped a crisp from a great height. 'You're new to this town, Calvin,' I said. 'I don't suppose you know that I'm a boy detective. I'm well known for solving crimes. But don't worry about it. You weren't to know.'

He was struck dumb. And when he recovered from the shock, he sat down on the grass next to me, all chummy like. 'What crime are you working on, Damian?' he said. 'Is it exciting?'

I tapped the side of my nose. 'Don't say a word,' I whispered, 'but the security team have asked me to watch out for criminal activity on the camp site. I'll be working undercover.'

I know this was a lie but Baggy-Pants was a real pain so it didn't count. I looked him right in the eye. 'Don't tell anybody what I'm doing,' I said. 'You might blow my cover.'

He nodded frantically. 'I won't say a word,' he said. 'I promise. You just act normal, Damian, as though you're an ordinary kid.'

It was then that Mum looked out of the Cookin' Shack and called me in. Goodbye, Calvin.

Back inside the Cookin' Shack, I was soon bogged down in the drudgery of unpacking boxes and filling the fridge. But when a man walked in and started talking to Mum, my detective's senses were suddenly on the alert. I stared at him and knew straightaway that this man was a criminal.

How did I know this?

Was it because he was tall? Was it because he was wearing an odd grey suit? No. It was because he had a bald patch.

You see, I had recently worked out a new theory of Criminal Types:

PEOPLE WITH BALD PATCHES ON TOP OF THEIR HEADS WERE DEFINITELY UP TO NO GOOD.

These types of criminal were very cunning and hard to track down as they often cover the bald patch by gluing strands of hair over it. But this man had been careless. His bald patch was clearly visible.

Luckily, Mum called me over and I was able to get a closer look at him.

'This is my son, Damian,' she said, smiling her posh smile. 'Damian, this is the site manager, Mr Wizzle.'

Mr Wizzle? What kind of name was that? A false one, I bet. Another reason to suspect him.

I amaze myself sometimes. I had only been here for half a day and I had already spotted a likely criminal.

Chapter 4

When Mr Wizzle had gone, I went outside to get my bike. I was just putting on my helmet when Calvin Baggy-Pants came running down the path. Oh no! Not again. I jumped inside the van, hoping that he wouldn't see me. But it was too late.

'Damian!' he yelled. 'I need your help.'

I wondered what he could possibly want with me – until he told me the shocking news.

'My bike's been stolen! My expensive new bike. It's gone.'

Now I understood.

Baggy-Pants was almost in tears. 'You will help, won't you?' he begged. 'Dad's reported the theft to Mr Wizzle – but he's useless. He doesn't seem to do anything.'

No wonder, I thought. Mr Wizzle was probably mixed up with a criminal gang.

'I'll help,' I said, smiling my wise detective's smile. 'If anyone can find your bike, I can.'

Calvin let out a four-star sigh of relief.

'What a piece of luck that you're here, Damian,' he said, and gave me a bar of chocolate.

Maybe he wasn't so bad after all, I thought. Maybe I'd judged him too harshly.

I took out my notebook and jotted down the facts.

name-Calvin
Bike-red and silver
Left on the grass
Value of bike
expensive

'I wish you'd called me sooner,' I said, snapping my notebook shut. 'The trail could have gone cold by now.'

He chewed on his bottom lip and looked pretty miserable. 'It's a brand new bike. I've only had it a week.'

'Don't worry,' I said. 'I have solved loads of crimes. Just stick with me. You might learn something.'

I asked him to take me back to his chalet and show me exactly where he had left the bike. I soon found a clue. It had been raining earlier that morning and the footpath was muddy. Right there in front of the chalet, was a set of tyre marks.

'Excellent,' I said. 'If my instincts are as brilliant as usual, these prints will lead us straight to the criminal.'

I marched off down the path with my

eyes fixed on the bike tracks until Calvin called, 'We've got company, Damian.'

I spun round to see a whole load of kids following us. There must have been ten or twelve or maybe more. Some were running. Some were riding bikes and one little girl had a small pink tricycle.

'We want to help find Calvin's bike,' they said. 'We know it's been stolen.'

They were obviously keen and gathered round in a group.

'Now listen,' I said. 'I am Damian

Drooth, supersleuth and ace detective. If you want to help me solve this crime you must swear to secrecy.'

'What's secrecy?' asked the small girl on the pink tricycle. (She was called Tilly.)

'You mustn't say a word about this to any grown-up.'

'I promise, Damian,' said Tilly.

And the others said, 'I promise.'

'I promise.'

'I promise.'

'Then I will swear you in as members of the Damian Drooth Detective School,' I said.

I made them hold up their hands and repeat the Detectives' Code:

I WILL ALWAYS LISTEN TO DAMIAN DROOTH AND FOLLOW HIS WISE INSTRUCTIONS

Then we all carried on down the path following the tyre prints in the mud. It was bad luck that the tracks grew fainter and fainter. And in the end, they disappeared altogether.

'In my opinion,' I said, pointing to the ground, 'the criminal got off the bike and pushed it onto the grass. Cunning.'

Then Tilly, who was standing some way from the rest of us, suddenly squealed. 'I've found another bike track and a footprint! Look! Look!'

I went over and saw that she was pointing towards a patch of mud in the grass.

Quickly, I took out my notebook and sketched the footprint. It was large – obviously a man's – and very unusual. With careful detective work, I would find out who was the owner of the shoe that made the print. I was certain that he was the man who had stolen Calvin's bike.

Chapter 5

'We must preserve this footprint at all cost,' I said to the team. 'It's a vital clue.'

I told them to stand round it, making sure that the evidence was not destroyed. Then I ran back to the Cookin' Shack.

'Damian,' said Mum, who was still doing the preparations for lunch, 'I've been waiting for you. Please wrap some knives and forks in the paper napkins, will you? That would be a real help.'

'Actually, Mum, I'm busy,' I said.

'Busy?' she snapped and gave me one of her looks. 'Come and help. Now!

I thought it best to do as she said and so I grabbed a few knives and forks and wrapped them up at lightning speed.

When Mum wasn't looking, I took my chance to get what I'd come for – a plastic tub big enough to cover the footprint. There were lots of tins and boxes of stuff and I found one full of flour that was just the right size.

I poured the flour into a carrier bag. A bit spilled on the floor – but not much. There was masses left.

Before Mum could find me another job to do, I slipped out of the hut and back to where the kids were standing in a circle, protecting the footprint.

'I got this,' I said, waving the tub over my head.

The kids started giggling.

'What?' I said.

'You look ever so funny, Damian,' said Tilly. 'Your hair's turned all white.'

I guessed there must have been a bit of flour left in the tub. So what?

Quickly, I bent down and covered the shoe print with the tub.

'That's really impressive, Damian,' Calvin said. 'What now?'

'We need camouflage*,' I said, 'so nobody will see it.'

*Camouflage *is what they do in the army. They stick leaves and twigs on their helmets so nobody can see them. But if they are in the desert, they spray glue all over their uniform and cover it with sand.*

We collected rocks and stones and piled them on top of the tub to stop it blowing away. Then we snapped some bits off the trees and covered them up.

'That's cool,' said Calvin. 'Nobody will notice it.'

I nodded. 'The evidence is safe,' I said. 'And when I catch the criminal, I'll show the footprint to the police.'

'Oh, Damian,' said Tilly, clapping her hands to her chest. 'You're very, very clever.'

Tilly may be small but she's an intelligent girl.

Chapter 6

The thief probably thought he'd got away with Calvin's bike. But he hadn't reckoned with yours truly, Damian Drooth. I had a cunning plan to catch him. I was going to lay a trap.

'I need to borrow your tricycle, Tilly,' I said. 'Is that OK?'

'Yes, you can, Damian,' she said, smiling right back at me. 'I want to help.'

'Thanks,' I said. 'You won't mind if it gets stolen, will you?'

 Suddenly, Tilly's eyes grew big as gobstoppers. She opened her mouth wide and let out a terrible cry and burst into tears.

It was ages before she calmed down. Anyway, when I explained that her tricycle was going to play a mega important part in capturing a serious criminal, she saw the sense of it.

But Calvin, who is not the brightest candle on the cake, didn't understand. 'Why borrow a tricycle, Damian? Why not a bike?'

I explained that the thief wouldn't be able to ride away on a tricycle. 'It would be too small for a grown-up.' It was pretty obvious to me.

I took Tilly's three wheeler and put it under an oak tree not far from the path. It was bright pink and sparkly so it would be easy for the bike thief to spot it.

'You all go into the wood,' I said to the kids. 'Hide behind those bushes.'

'Then what?' Calvin asked.

I tapped my nose and winked. 'Just wait and watch,' I said.

While Calvin went off with the others, I climbed up the oak tree. I wriggled out along a branch until I was right over Tilly's trike. All I had to do was to hang on until the criminal arrived.

I didn't have to wait long.

First, I heard footsteps. Then, through the leaves, I saw a man approaching. I couldn't see his face but I could tell he had no taste in clothes.

 He was wearing sandals and socks and baggy camouflage shorts over his hairy legs. He looked absolutely ridiculous.

He must have seen the tricycle under the tree because he left the path and walked towards it. When he bent down to look at it more closely, that was when I saw the top of his head.

He had a bald patch. Not a huge one – but big enough to show that he must be a crook.

The man looked over his shoulder to see if there was anyone around. Of course he couldn't see me up in the tree.

Just as I thought, he grabbed hold of Tilly's precious pink tricycle. I acted at once and flung myself off the branch. I yelled and spread my arms wide like an eagle in full flight. THUNK! I landed on top of him.

'Aaaaaagggghhhhh!' he screamed as he collapsed under me and fell face down in the grass.

'Hey, you guys!' I shouted to the kids. 'Come and help. I've got him.'

Calvin and the others came bursting out of their hiding place and flung themselves on top of the bike thief. It looked like a heap of swarming ants. The bike thief was squashed flat on the ground.

Tilly was so excited that I had saved her bike that she flung her arms round my neck and tried to kiss me.

YUK!

But I managed to push her away.

'Don't let the thief move,' I said to the kids. 'I need to check his shoes.'

I walked round to his feet, dragged one sandal off and looked at the sole. Did it match the footprint in the mud? Would I be able to solve the crime? I took out my notebook and looked at the sketch I had made.

'Is it him?' asked Calvin, who was sitting on the man's head.

I checked the drawing again. After all my efforts . . . No. It was not a match. We had got the wrong man.

It happens sometimes.

'OK, guys,' I said. 'Let him go. He must be an innocent passer-by, even though he was behaving in a very suspicious manner.'

The kids were disappointed but they stood up and stepped back.

'What's going on?' the man barked as he raised his head out of the grass. For the first time I saw his face, beard and all. I was shocked. It was none other than Inspector Crockitt, the head of our local police force.

Chapter 7

'What on earth are you up to, Damian?' Inspector Crockitt said as he struggled to his feet and tried to recover his breath. (I don't think he's quite as fit as he should be.)

'We thought you were a thief,' I explained.

He should have understood but I don't think he did. He pressed his lips together like he does when he's annoyed. 'I wasn't stealing that tricycle, you stupid boy,' he said. 'I was going to take it to lost property.'

I thought it best that we should talk in private so I led him away from the others.

'There's a bike thief about,' I whispered. 'But I expect you know that already. I suppose you've come here to work undercover?'

His face turned red. 'No, I am NOT undercover!' he snapped. 'I'm trying to have a quiet holiday with my family and you, Damian Drooth, are . . .'

You won't be interested in what he said next. He ranted on for ages. I think he was just having a bad day.

Of course, the kids were dying to know what we were talking about.

'Oh do tell us, Damian,' said Tilly, when he'd gone.

'Secret stuff,' I said. 'He was impressed by what I'd found out already.'

This was not exactly a lie as I knew Inspector Crockitt *would* have been impressed *if* he'd given me the chance to tell him.

'So what now?' asked Calvin.

'I've got a plan B,' I said.

'What's that?'

'The thief takes bikes, right?' I said.

'RIGHT,' all the kids agreed.

'Then we all get our bikes and smear honey on them,' I explained. 'When the thief comes along and takes one, he'll be covered in it. See? Simple.'

'Won't he just wash it off?' said Calvin, which was negative, I thought.

But Tilly came up with an intelligent idea. 'We could mix blueberries in it,' she said. 'They make lovely blue stains and it's ever so difficult to get off.'

'Good brain work, Tilly,' I said. 'And I know where I can find blueberries. There's a box of them in Mum's fridge. I don't suppose she'll miss them.'

The kids went off to get their bikes and I sneaked into the Cookin' Shack. Mum was still cutting sandwiches.

To make sure she didn't see me, I did my SAS manoeuvre, wriggling on my stomach across the floor. I have practised this in the back garden loads of time. It's a very useful technique.

Without being spotted, I reached the shelves where the jars of honey were kept. I took four of them and then I crawled across to the fridge and took out the box of blueberries. Success!

Outside, most of the kids had returned with their bikes. I mixed the honey and blueberries and spread it on the handlebars and seats.

No problem – except for a little kid called Jack who started crying when I put the stuff on his bike. He went into a right tizz. Beating his fists. Stamping his feet. There was no stopping him.

When all the bikes were covered in the purple honey, I gave the kids instructions to go and leave them outside their chalets.

'The thief is sure to come along and take at least one of them,' I explained. 'Then we must keep our eyes open for someone who has hands covered with purple honey.'

Another crime would be solved in no time.

Chapter 8

While the kids were heading back to their chalets, I had a serious chat with Calvin.

'I don't believe that Inspector Crockitt is on holiday,' I said. 'I think he's here undercover. I'm going to find him and tell him about the honey trap. He'll be really interested in my brilliant plan.'

Calvin agreed. 'You go and find him,' he said. 'I'll be going back to the chalet. This detective work is exhausting.'

I set off to look for Inspector Crockitt and found him sitting on a towel near the swimming pool. He was wearing sunglasses and some stupid flowery shorts. I suppose this was his disguise.

I sat down next to him and began to explain my plot to catch the bike thief. But he pretended to be reading his book.

'Why don't you have a swim, Damian?' he said eventually.

But it was important that I stayed. I was giving him my top-secret information, when a big guy with a bald head and fierce black eyebrows came rushing into the pool area. He was mad – shouting and ranting and waving his arms. Worst of all, this dangerous man was heading towards Inspector Crockitt. I had to do something.

I leapt between the big guy and the Inspector.

'Stop!' I said, holding up my hand. 'This man is an officer of the Law.'

But the man kept coming. He even tried to dodge round me, which was a big mistake as the surface was very wet. His foot slipped and – of course – he fell sideways into the swimming pool. SPLASH! Was it any wonder? All kids know you should never run near swimming pools.

I was amazed. Even when we'd saved the man's life by dragging him out of the pool, he was still angry. He stood there dripping and yelling at Inspector Crockitt. It turned out that he was the dad of the boy called Jack.

'You want to control this son of yours,' he screamed, pointing at me. 'Tell him to stay away from my little boy. He's covered his bike in purple honey. He's very upset.'

Inspector Crockitt tried to explain that I wasn't his son. But Jack's dad wouldn't listen. He carried on shouting and bellowing at the top of his voice.

So I thought I'd better disappear.

Chapter 9

I ran back to the Cookin' Shack. It was nearly time for lunch and I was starving.

When I walked in, I was shocked to see Mum talking to the site manager, Mr Wizzle, who was a possible suspect for the bike robbery (on account of his bald patch).

Mum looked across at me. 'I was just telling Mr Wizzle that I've had some things stolen,' she said. 'Some flour and four jars of honey and a box of blueberries. You don't know anything about it, do you, Damian?'

Luckily, I didn't have to reply as the door swung open and people began to flock in and queue up for their lunch.

When they'd all been served and I was sneaking a sausage sandwich for myself, an old man limped in.

'Sorry I'm late,' he said as he collected his food. 'I've just been to see the nurse.'

I could see he was in a terrible state. He had a plaster stuck across his nose and a bandage on his head.

'Oh dear, what happened?' Mum asked.

The man's wife, who looked very cross, answered. 'It's disgusting,' she said and banged her fist on the counter. 'My husband was riding through the wood, minding his own business, when he crashed. Somebody had deliberately put a pile of stones in the middle of the path and covered it with leaves. That's dangerous, if you ask me. It ought not to be allowed.'

I was shocked. The old man had smashed into the tub I had placed over the footprint. What a disaster! Our evidence was ruined. My only hope was that the purple honey mixture would help me catch the crook.

The Cookin' Shack was the perfect place to be on lookout. Anyone coming in for lunch after stealing a bike would have stains on his hands. It would be impossible to wash them off. I immediately offered to clear the tables so I could check for give-away marks. Cunning, eh?

But maybe I was too keen. Maybe I was a bit too quick at taking away the plates.

'Hey! I haven't finished,' the old man shouted, waving his knife and fork in the air.

Bad luck that Mum heard and came rushing over.

'Thank you, Damian,' she said in that voice she uses when she's really angry but she can't shout at me because somebody's near. 'Go and get things ready for coffee, will you, please?'

I tried to protest.

'Thank you, Damian. Now!'

I slumped away, misunderstood as usual. I hadn't had time to see any purple marks. My plan was wrecked.

I went over to arrange the coffee cups on the table which was next to the store cupboard. On the floor, right in front of it, was the white flour I'd spilled earlier.

I was thinking of sweeping it up. But before I could, a tall man, wearing black trousers and a white T-shirt, walked in and headed in my direction.

'Give us a cup of coffee, will yer, kid?' he said. 'I've been on duty all morning.'

I noticed he had a badge on his shoulder with the word SECURITY on it.

I leaned forward and whispered, 'Been looking out for the bike thief, have you?' This was by way of friendly conversation. After all, we had a lot in common. We were both in the business of protecting the public.

But for some reason, the security guard suddenly looked nervous and his mouth started twitching. I was suspicious and kept my eyes fixed on him as I poured his coffee. This was not easy and I think I spilled a bit.

'Don't bother,' he said. 'I've changed my mind.' He hurried out of the dining room, leaving the coffee behind.

It was then that I glanced down and I saw something amazing. His footprint was there, clear as daylight, pressed into the flour. Immediately, I pulled out my drawing of the shoe print and checked it against the one on the floor.

It was a perfect match!

Chapter 10

I abandoned the coffee table and raced outside. I looked one way and the other only to find that the security guard was already out of sight. There was only one thing to do.

I ran back into the Cookin' Shack and shouted.

'CODE RED. CODE RED. EMERGENCY! NOW!'*

There was a buzz around the room and everybody looked up. Of course my team of trainee detectives knew how to react. They immediately dropped their knives and forks, pushed back their chairs and raced over to me, regardless of the obstacles in their way. One or two chairs were knocked down and somebody's dad fell over. But nothing serious.

*CODE RED *is what they have in the army when somebody really dangerous is shooting at them. Nobody was shooting at us but it was a good thing to shout.*

While the adults were in a state of panic, I ran outside and the kids followed me.

'I have proof that a security guard stole the bike,' I announced.

Before I could say more, I saw Calvin running down the path towards us.

'Have I missed lunch?' he gasped. 'I was reading my comic.' I filled him in on what had happened.

'DAMIAN!' he said, as if he'd been struck by lightning. 'I've just seen that security guard. He walked past our chalet as I was leaving – honest! He was heading towards the wood.'

'Right,' I said, looking at the eager faces of the kids. 'Grab your bikes. We're on our way.'

By that time, the adults were pouring out of the dining room to find out what was going on. But we were soon

pedalling frantically towards the wood (all except Calvin who didn't have a bike). It wasn't long before we saw the thief walking ahead of us.

At once, I yelled, 'STOP in the name of the Law!'

The thief spun round and a look of horror spread across his face as he saw us kids racing towards him like a pack of hounds.

'NO!' he shouted and started to run.

But he was very unfit. He was panting and gasping for breath and, before long, we caught up with him.

'Surround him, guys!' I shouted and they made a circle with their bikes so that the security guard was left crouching and quaking in the middle.

Then the adults arrived soon after. Most of them were red-faced and out of puff. But in the lead was none other than Inspector Crockitt.

'What are you up to now, Damian?' he asked.

I pointed to the security guard. 'This,' I said, 'is the thief who stole Calvin's bike AND I HAVE PROOF.'

Mum came pushing through the crowd. 'Oh, Damian!' she said. 'You're not playing at detectives again, are you? Can't you just be a normal boy?'

She was embarrassing me big time.

But Mr Wizzle (who turned out not to be a crook) was close behind her. 'Just a minute, Mrs Drooth,' he interrupted. 'Let me ask your son a few questions. He might have something here.'

I answered his questions all right. I even showed him the drawing in my notebook. I could tell he was impressed.

He turned to the security guard. 'What have you got to say about this?' he asked.

The thief, surrounded by so many tough-looking kids, confessed immediately. 'I'll show you where I hid the bike. Just get me away from this lot,' he sobbed.

Another case solved.

Chapter 11

The adults were an ungrateful bunch. I'd solved a crime brilliantly but they said I had led their kids astray. Why? Just because I had used their bikes as decoys. Just because they were covered in purple sticky stuff. Just because some of the kids got a little itsy bit on their clothes.

I tried to explain but it was useless.

Worst of all, Mum was in a really, really bad mood. On a scale of 1 to 10, her bad mood registered 15. For the rest of the week, she wouldn't let me out of her sight.

'Inspector Crockitt doesn't want you following him around,' she told me. 'You've been pestering him all day. He's got a right to have a holiday, you know.'

But I was suspicious. I still believed he was working under cover.

The only person who was really grateful for my detective work was Calvin.

'Thanks, Damian,' he said. 'That bike's worth a fortune. You're a pal. Next week, why don't you come round to our house and swim in our pool? We've a billiard table, too, so we can play, if you want.'

It turned out that Calvin wasn't bad for a spoiled rich kid. In fact, he could be a really good buddy.